Date Due

SHADOWS
Text and illustrations © 1987 by John Canty

For information address
Harper & Row Junior Books, 10 East 53rd Street,
New York, N.Y. 10022.
**Published simultaneously in Canada
by Fitzhenry & Whiteside Limited, Toronto.**

Library of Congress Cataloging-in-Publication Data
Canty, John.
  Shadows.

  Summary: A young boy's nighttime world of mysterious
shadows disappears when he decides to be brave and
confront the dark.
  [1. Bedtime—Fiction.   2. Night—Fiction.   3. Fear—Fiction]   1. Title.
PZ7.C17358Sh 1987   [E]   87-205
ISBN 0-06-020988-7

Created and produced by
Sadie Fields Productions Ltd, London.

Printed and bound in Italy.

First American Edition

Shadows

John Canty

Harper & Row, Publishers

Benjamin hates the dark.
Fierce creatures live there.

Late at night
he sees one move.
Or at least he thinks he does.

He looks deeper
into the darkness,

black and silent.
But nothing appears.

Benjamin knows it's there,
watching him.

He makes a shadow with his hands.

Black to furry gray it grows
and springs to life from wall to floor

to hide beneath a chair.

Benjamin looks, but only finds
a mysterious shadow growing on the wall.

Benjamin watches it grow bigger.

He runs until he reaches the door.
"If I run," he says aloud,
"it will always chase me.

Always and forever.
But this is my room, and I won't
run from anything!"

So Benjamin turns.
All around him shadows whirl and swirl,
then melt away.

They vanish into the farthest corners,
back to where dark shadows belong.

The night is quiet once again.
Benjamin yawns. Back in bed,
he falls asleep in the friendly darkness,

safe and brave,
again to dream.